SPEEDY WHEELS

William Bumble

SCHOLASTIC INC.

New York Toronto London Auckland Sydney

Contents

Introduction

The inventors of the bike and the car would be astounded at the way in which their prized possessions have developed. For they have far exceeded their original notion of being a safe comfortable means of transport. These machines are now capable of just about anything!

First, there are the real 'toughies', machines capable of racing through deep mud, up rocky hillsides, down near vertical slopes, before scrambling across swirling streams. The drivers have to be every bit as tough as their vehicles, and only the most determined and skillful succeed.

Different sides to today's bikes. Showbiz and stunts (top left), as eyecatching as the customized bike (below). But if it's real speed your prefer, there's nothing to beat a racing bike.

Racing drivers take tremendous risks, in addition to being under enormous pressure from the public, press, and sponsors. See the scarry look in the eyes of this driver (right) as he prepares for a race. It's no wonder that when his rival takes the checkered flag his team mates respond with wild excitement.

Then there are the machines made to amaze. They can 'leap' or 'fly' over the deepest canyon, or 'catapult' over the longest row of buses you have ever seen. Needless to say these machines don't last long, and often break up on landing!

The owners of fast, customized bikes would be horrified if their vehicles were ever damaged. They've perfected the art of turning bikes into art. Just look at the engine on page 6 to see how this can be transformed into beautiful, extraordinary shapes.

But the real surprise to the early inventors would be today's Grand Prix racers. Designed by the finest experts, using the latest space technology, at enormous cost, they have produced the ultimate in 'speedy wheels'. They guarantee their championship winning drivers 'Hollywood' stardom and lifestyle to match. It's a long cry from the time when cars and bikes were being laughed off the streets as 'the machines that would never last'.

Kings of the Road

Versatility is the name of the game. Just ask the owner of a fast, customized bike. See how he's transformed it into a magnificent, show-stopping collector's piece — a bike guaranteed to look better than the rest.

But speed and glamor don't always go hand-in-hand. Take the bikes driven by the police. They might not look as good as the customized bike, but they can certainly travel. And they've got enough signs and extras to warn people that they are coming!

There are plenty of cars that combine power and good looks. Right at the top of the range are Porsche, Mercedes, Jaguar, and BMW. All have fantastically luxurious interiors with all the latest gadgetry, including top-performance hi-fi. But they also have engines capable of exceeding the speed limit in practically every country in the world. Yet while these Kings of the Road can't be pushed to the limit, the sheer thrill of driving such powerful beasts makes up for having to go rather more slowly than their owners would want!

When is a bike a work of art? When it's a Harley-Davidson (below), complete with a dazzling, gold-plated twin engine. Though less ornate, this Suzuki (far left) has got enough power crammed into its engine to satisfy any bike enthusiast.

Top right: *The Camaro is one of the gutsiest cars around. Based on the Ford Mustang, it has gradually won its fight for popularity. A recent major development was the world-beating IROC Camaro.*

Below right: *The super sleek Porsche 928, with adjustable headlights and every comfort you could hope to find in a car.*

Center right: *The Mercedes-Benz C111 was the smash hit of the 1969 Frankfurt Car Show. Just one look at the gull wings will tell you why. However, the fashion never caught on, and is now rarely seen.*

Superbikes

Top
The extremeley impressive Honda VF1000, fired by a V4 engine.

The furious search for extra speed was given a tremendous boost in the 1980s with the development of the turbo. It thrusts every last bit of raw firepower back through the engine in a bid to ensure that no source of energy is wasted. And in the fierce competition between manufacturers of top-class road bikes, they even introduced 'on-board' computers to control the fuel injection in a major bid to leave nothing to chance.

As the great headline-catching Grand Prix bikes get ever more sophisticated, it is inevitable that their design systems will gradually filter down through the bike hierarchy. This has created another class of bike, the superbike, for the 'ace engine cowboys' who can outride and outperform most of the competition on the city streets.

It also means that the 'cowboys' can get a real feel of what it is like to thrust down the final straight at full speed in front of a 100,000 crowd. And with these machines capable of overtaking at 150 mph it's certain only the best amateur riders can handle this. Designed to scorch along like a rocket tearing through the atmosphere, the future of the superbike looks unbeatable.

Below
In the 1980s the quest for extra speed produced the turbo. Note, **far left**, the unremarkable looking engine for the Kawasaki 750 turbo which, as anyone who has ever ridden it will testify, is in fact one of the most remarkable bikes around.

Above
Vision of things to come. Honda's exclusive 1200 cc Gold Wing Aspencade has just about every luxury you could hope to find on a bike, including loudspeakers!

Sport and Speed

There are many kinds of car race, but the ones the crowds really pack in to see are those for specially designed Grand Prix cars, and for sports cars and modified sedans, featured here.

For the well and truly modified sedan there's nothing to beat NACASR's challenging circuit. The Europeans however, tend to prefer races between cars which have the same size engine and structure in a bid to find the top drivers. And for those drivers who really enjoy punishment, there's always the shattering, unsparing 24-hour Le Mans with its 621 miles of furious French endurance.

Below: Take one ordinary car, add a snarling high-powered engine, plenty of reinforcement and a driver with guts, and you can take on the best. Here a Mini, bored with life on the freeway, gives a fast thrilling ride when going flat out in competition.

Left: A constant headache for race organizers is how to let the crowds get close to the action, while guaranteeing their safety. Here, at Le Mans, there are clearly no problems, with the spectators well back and high above the race track.

Below: *You don't need the latest model for a first-rate race, as shown by this line-up of MGs at Brands Hatch, England.*

Above: *The Dodge Charger. Despite various design changes in a bid for speedway success, it never really made it to the top.*

Racing Triumphs

When a Grand Prix comes to town it's big business. It's not just the drivers who are involved — there are hundreds of highly skilled, hand-picked mechanics, anxious managers, eagle-eyed backers, wives and children, journalists and TV crews desperate for a quote, and celebrities galore, from 'J.R. Ewing' to royalty!

Being a World Championship racing driver means being super fit, both to drive and travel, right round the world. Here (left) Nelson Piquet and designer Gordon Murray discuss their car and race plan at the Detroit Grand Prix. Nothing can be left to chance.

Then it's onto the track (above) and time to put theory into practice. But no matter what the level of competition or size of crowd there's only one thing that counts. Being first past the flag (far right). From then on, for the determined, skillful, and perhaps lucky winner (and runners up), there's only one way to celebrate. Alain Prost and Keke Rosberg (top) show how to do it, in style.

Thousands of people are on the move during the World Championship season, all, no matter what their role, trying to work out who is going to win. For at the end, when it's time to pack up, it's the winner who goes down in history. Even those who repeatedly come very close to glory find that defeat counts for nothing. For England's Nigel Mansell in 1986, when he had two glorious chances to snatch the title, failing both times, huge checks for the runners-up are no compensation. Triumph is all that counts!

Grand Prix and Speedway Stars

Center: Eddie Lawson (No. 4), Randy Mamola (3), and Barry Sheene (7), are seen furiously pursuing Ron Haslam (9).

Bottom: Phil Read, the English star who first hit the world headlines back in 1962. One of the country's most successful racers, he took major honors at 125, 250, and 500cc, right through to the 1970s.

Early bike races were long, tough and demanding. Some lasted up to four or five hours, consuming 300-mile circuits. Later came the division into different cc classes, and in 1938 the European Championships. The first World Championship, as we know is today, came in 1949. And with it came the emergence of the great bike manufacturers and the star riders.

World-wide press coverage of all the major events has meant that the riders seen on these pages, and the champions such as Marco Luchinelli, Barry Sheene, Eddie Lawson and Kenny Roberts, get the recognition they deserve. They've got skill and nerve. But they've also got to know when to say 'No'. At the 1979 Belgian Grand Prix the race organizers insisted the wet new circuit was not dangerous. The stars knew better and staged a walkout. If you're going to get to the top and, more importantly, stay there, you've got to combine skill, nerve, a love of high speed and good race tactics with excellent common sense.

Eddie Lawson (USA) — 1984 World Champion.

Randy Mamola (USA) — three times just failing to be No. 1.

'Rocket' Ron Haslam (England) — many good wins, but not in the World Championship.

Above: The American 750cc events include some of the toughest around, with the most successful riders being guaranteed stardom.

Freddie Spencer (USA)
— 1983, 500cc World
Champion.

Carlos Lavado (Venezuela)
— 1983, 250cc World
Champion.

Racing Disasters

It doesn't matter how far drivers 'rehearse' their every move, again and again in the last few days before a major race, things don't always go to plan!

Take the start of a recent Grand Prix when unbelievably one of the officials was still on the track, as the car engines roared like B-52 bombers, awaiting take-off. Millions worldwide saw him crouching between two cars as the lights turned green. But the drivers didn't. Fortunately this was not a major disaster involving half the field, fire and death, but it does show you can take nothing for granted, in any event, whether driving cars or bikes.

And who are the bravest of the two kinds of driver? While the car offers some protection it also means you're sitting just inches away from the explosive gas tank. Bike drivers, on the other hand, run the risk of being catapulted through the air at 200 mph. An extraordinary spectacle for spectators, but it sure isn't fun for the human missile!

Fire (right) — the most terrifying sight to a racing driver. Although cars are now designed to minimize the fire risk, once it breaks out it can just be a matter of seconds before there's a terrifying explosion.

Another kind of disaster (above) - falling behind in the race as the wheels sink ever deeper into the sand.

Two drivers in a fix. Marc Surer (below) spins off the track to the amazement of the spectators, who are well protected by a secure safety barrier. But there's no one on hand to help this unfortunate driver (below left) who is dazed after a fall in the Paris-Dakar desert race.

Stunts and Supercross

Anyone who has ever ridden a bike knows that there's more to life than racing. The world's top stunt rider Evel Knievel certainly knows that. For him, and his fellow daredevils, the bike is showbiz at its most spectacular.

If there's a canyon, they'll blast their way across. If there's an endless row of buses or cars, they'll soar high over them. Nothing beats the challenge, the chance to prove that the seemingly impossible is no problem at all.

It's no wonder that wherever characters like Evel Knievel perform huge crowds turn out to see whether he will succeed, or have to be helped out of the wreckage!

Those who dream of one day performing such incredible feats need somewhere to perfect their skills. And where better than on a supercross course. It involves well organized events, all manner of obstacles, mid-air leaps and high-speed crashes. Only the best survive!

Below: *Supercross star Paul Hunt keeps his eyes firmly on his landing spot, though it's not all that clear if Archie Nyquist (**near right**) knows where he's bound. Note the size of his powerful bike. It takes precision judgement to balance it at that anglel, without toppling backwards.*

Far right (top three): *It's head down and straight on, even if there is a brick wall in the way!*

Bottom right: *One for the future. A 'Red Helmet' leaps through a blazing hoop of fire.*

Mudpluggers and Motorcross

For those who prefer natural obstacles, rather than those constructed by man, try 'mudplugging'. You'll find yourself having to drive over just about everything the rest of us would do anything to avoid — streams filled with rocks, thick bogs, sand dunes, dense woodland, and the steepest hillsides imaginable.

Not surprisingly the bikes have to be specially adapted to these tough conditions. And the riders have to skillfully manipulate every problem, without resorting to regaining their balance by putting their feet on the ground. For that is when vital points are deducted.

Motorcross is similarly demanding. One of the main problems is skidding on the rough circuit. This is certainly good fun for the spectators, but not for the drivers. Their bikes have powerful engines. Unlike the 'mudpluggers' which are small, and have up to six gears.

If you want a different approach to racing, mudplugging and motorcross could be the answer. But you've got to be rough and tough for these sports, and capable of keeping control of your bike no matter how difficult the conditions.

Mud is certainly one major difficulty, whether you're out on your own *(below)* or following the leader along a narrow trail *(below right)*. Either way it's because if you slow down too much you're likely to get well and truly bogged down. No wonder the young would-be World Champion *(right)* is wondering what he's let himself in for. Because if it isn't the mud, it's snow and water *(top left and center left)*.

Drag Racing

Drag racing began in the 1920s, since then it's become a spectacular, all-American specialization. It's the motorbike rider's equivalent of lifting off from Cape Kennedy. Huge 'muscular' engines 'blast' rider and machine down a quarter mile straight runway at lightning speed. As the hundreds of spectators wait for the 'Go', the excitement is intense.

And it's the same when watching the extraordinary coffin-like drag cars. They too are propelled by huge roaring engines, only they are placed perilously close to the driver's neck! The cars front and rear wheels could not be more dissimilar, and come as quite a surprise to newcomers to the sport. Those at the back are giants, the real moving force, while those at the front of the car's elegant 'nose' are more bicycle wheels: small, thin and completely dwarfed.

One of the skills in handling these powerful cars is the ability to withstand the sudden, immense surge of speed from a standing start . . . and, of course, knowing how to stop it when you cross the finish line!

Above: Everyone stands well back when cars like this are in action.

Below: The 'Team Big Spender' give rider and Kawasaki the final 'once over' before they hurtle down the track.

Top left and below left: The bikes are different, but the riding style is exactly the same. Straight back and strong grip.

The World's Fastest Wheels

As the drivers wait on the grid for the green light, winning is the first priority. But to win and hit the record books as the world's fastest racing driver would be even better!

Yet it does not matter how good a driver you are, how strong your nerves are, how willing you are to take risks and overtake when others hold back, in the end you're only as good as your machine. The better, more efficient and reliable it is, the more chance you've got of becoming a racing superstar. That's why each team regularly spends a fortune on seeking out the best design, whether it be for a car or bike. Records are made not only on the track, but behind the scenes.

Record breaker Rob McElnea (far left) almost 'flying' to an Isle of Man average speed of 118mph. But could this design (near left) be the shape of tomorrow's superbike?

Hair pin bends (below right) make for exciting contests, but drivers in search of the record books prefer wide open spaces (center right) for real acceleration.

Fast Machines from the Past

For as long as people have owned cars and bikes, they have raced them. But advances made by designers, particularly over the past three decades, have been so great that it's sometimes hard to realize that some of the early machines were specifically built for speed. Many of the cars look, as one of today's leading drivers recently said, 'like bath-tubs on wheels!'

But fast they were and surprisingly reliable. These early races tended to be held over huge distances on highways, and on the round small circuits we are familiar with today. One of the longest car races was between Paris and Peking!

Looking at the earlier of these pictures, and how dated the machines now seem, one wonders what the sports cars and bikes of tomorrow will look like? And how fast will *they* be able to go?

Two early machines from 1910. **Top left**: *a Matchless, ridden by Charlie Collier, an early star of the Isle of Man TT races. And* **top right** *a Linon Sport. Note the delightful antique horn by the rider's right hand!*

Left: *The Rover-BRM, complete with gas turbine, which finished in tenth place in the 1965 Le Mans race. The car was driven by two of Britain's greatest ever racing drivers, Graham Hill and Jackie Stewart.*

Above: A 1950's Moto-Guzzi,
still in excellent
working order.

Left: Juan-Manuel Fangio
gets a superb view of
Monaco harbor.

Carting

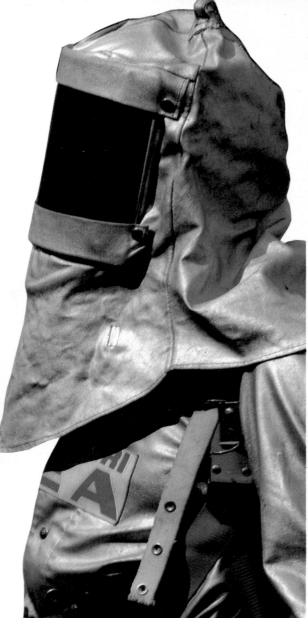

If you dream of one day becoming a champion racing driver, there's no better way to start your career than by kart racing. Although you won't find yourself breaking any speed records, you will acquire the vital basic driving skills.

And once you've passed this hurdle, you could find yourself competing for the prestigious CART championship. And that means driving in front of packed crowds, being surrounded by teams of mechanics and getting a real 'feel' of what it's like to be competing for a World Championship.

The Indianapolis 500 is the most highly regarded CART race. Its streamlined banked track enables drivers to exceed speed of 200 mph. So even at this level you've got to be fit, confident, skillful, and know how to look after yourself.

Top: *Dirt tracks, karts, small engines — and tremendous fun. This is where future champions learn their trade.*

Opposite, top left and right: *CART racing at Indianapolis. Color and excitement there may be, but the 'big time' also involves risks. The car engines use methanol instead of gasoline, which has a near 'invisible' flame. That's why officials in flame-proof clothing are a 'must' in case there's a terrible accident.*

Far left and above: *Despite the danger, nothing beats the thrill of racing round the track at full speed, particularly when it's banked for high speed.*

Off-Road Racing

For those who can't stop racing, even indoors, why not try radio-controlled model automobiles. These models aren't kids toys. They are extremely sophisticated scaled-down cars that look just like the real thing. They come in all shapes and sizes. You can buy large wagons that will climb over even the most demanding course, and the racers, including Formula 1, and sports cars and sedans. A good store should stock everything from Porsche 956 turbo, to a BMW turbo, Mercedes 300E, and a Ferrari.

The course can be as long and as difficult as you care to make it. You could even send away for a plan of your favorite track and try to reproduce it, scaled down of course! The average sized track of the real enthusiast is about 150 yards. But if that sounds huge, remember that these electronically controlled cars can reach speeds of 20 to 25 mph. Scaled up, that means they are doing the equivalent of nearly 200 mph. The cars rarely have all the gears, but will take one at a time. So, if your course is full of twists and turns, with new straight runs, then you can insert a low gear. If the track is going to be built for speed, then you need a high gear.

A contrast in styles. **Top right:** *A 'Porsche 911 turbo', and* **below,** *a vehicle for the extremely demanding surface. You can make the course as rough and tough as you like, with boulders and shallow streams, but those wheels should see it through.*

You can make up your own rules, but usually the races are held over five minutes, the winner being the car that has managed the most laps. If you prefer something more dramatic however, why not try drag racing. The track is just 40 yards, but the cars can reach a top speed of 65 mph.

Above: From a distance you might think this is the real thing, but in fact it's a very skilfully designed model. 'Formula 1' cars like this come with a hand-held radio control unit, enabling you to control the speed and direction (forward, reverse, left and right). There is also a speed gear selector switch, depending on whether you have constructed a track for low or high speeds.

31

A Minimedia Book, designed and produced by Multimedia
Books Ltd, 32-34 Gordon House Road, London NW5 1LP,
England

Copyright © 1988 Multimedia Books Ltd

First published in 1988 by Scholastic Inc., 730 Broadway, New
York, NY 10003

Designer: John Strange
Production: Zivia Desai

ISBN 0-590-41996-X

Origination by J Film Process Co Ltd., Bangkok, Thailand
Printed in Spain by Mateu Cromo